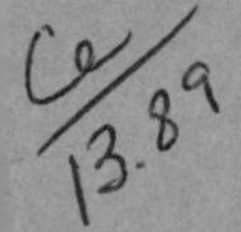

Byars, Betsy

The seven treasure hunts

$13.89

DATE			

The Seven Treasure Hunts

The Seven Treasure Hunts

by Betsy Byars
illustrated by Jennifer Barrett

HarperCollinsPublishers

Portions published previously in *Cricket* magazine.

THE SEVEN TREASURE HUNTS

Printed in the United States of America. For information address HarperCollins Children's Books, a division of HarperCollins Publishers, 10 East 53rd Street, New York, NY 10022.
3 4 5 6 7 8 9 10

Library of Congress Cataloging-in-Publication Data
Byars, Betsy Cromer.
The seven treasure hunts / by Betsy Byars ; illustrated by Jennifer Barrett.
p. cm.
Summary: Two boys make up a series of treasure hunts for each other, with disastrous and hilarious results.
ISBN 0-06-020885-6. — ISBN 0-06-020886-4 (lib. bdg.)
[1. Treasure hunt—Fiction. 2. Friendship—Fiction.]
I. Barrett, Jennifer, ill. II. Title.
PZ7.B9836Se 1991 90-32043
[Fic]—dc20 CIP
AC

Contents

Chapter One

The Hunt for the Secret Treasure

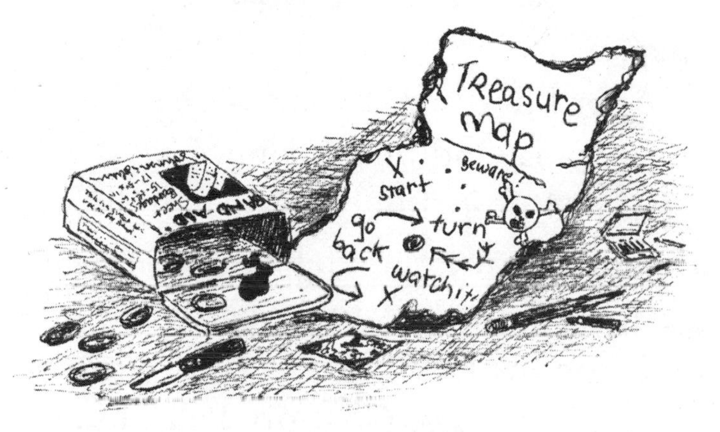

Last Saturday Goat and I hid treasures for each other to find. My treasure was seven pennies, a knife with one blade, a decal, and a balloon, all stuffed in a Band-Aid box. I buried it in a pot of flowers on my front porch.

Then I made a map that was very

tricky. It would lead Goat all over the neighborhood. And not only was it tricky, it looked like a real pirate map. I had drawn it on brown paper and burned the edges. I was proud of that map.

After I finished, I went to the corner where Goat and I had planned to meet. Goat had probably been busy hiding a treasure for me and making a map, and he looked pleased too. He had a big smile on his face.

"Here you go, Goat my Pal," I said.

I handed him my map. He handed me a dirty scrap of paper.

"What's this?" I asked.

"Clues."

"Clues? You were supposed to draw a map." I looked at the piece of paper. It was so little, it was hard to read.

Finally I made it out:

4 to the right. 6 to the left. 7 across. 1 ahead. 2 sideways. Look up.

"What's this, Goat?" I asked again, but Goat was already running down the sidewalk.

It looked to me as if he were heading straight for my house, straight for the pot of flowers.

4 to the right. Quickly I took four steps to the right. *6 to the left.* I did that. *7 across, 1 ahead, 2 sideways.*

I looked up. All I could see were some clouds in the sky.

"Goat!" I ran after him. When I got to my house, he was standing on the porch. He was pulling my mom's pansies out of the pot, spilling the dirt all over.

He reached in and came up with the Band-Aid box.

"Ta-daaaa!" he said.

"Goat, you didn't even use the map. I spent all morning on that map!"

"I didn't need it," Goat said. "I saw a piece of pansy on your watch—look, right there. Then I knew—you hid it in the old pansy pot."

I felt cheated.

"That's not fair," I said. "You were supposed to use the map!"

"I would have if I had needed it. Did you find your treasure yet?"

He knew I hadn't.

"No."

"Too tricky, huh, Jackie?"

"I haven't even had a chance to read the clues yet."

I glanced down at the piece of paper, pretending I was looking at it for the first time. "It's not so tricky."

"It's trickier than yours," Goat said. He stuck my mom's pansies back into the pot. He opened the Band-Aid box and shook out the contents.

He said, "Money—I can use that." He put it in his pocket. "A broken knife—"

"It's not broken."

"It's only got one blade."

"Well, it still cuts. Look!" I showed him a scar on my thumb.

"A decal that came from a cereal box—I know because I eat the same kind. And a balloon that says *I was a good patient.* I know where you got that, from our dentist. He stopped giving them to me because I bit him.

"Well, go ahead. Find your treasure."

I stared back at him. All week I had been looking forward to hiding treasures. Now he had ruined it. I opened my front door. "I'm bored with this."

"So, Jackie, it's too tough for you, huh? Go ahead and quit."

"I'm not quitting."

"Then find the treasure. I want to see

if you can do it."

"All right!" I stamped down the steps, down the sidewalk. Goat followed. I could hear him flipping the top of the metal box open and shut.

"You have to start at the corner," he said.

"I know where to start."

"Just being helpful," he said.

We walked to the corner without saying anything. I kept looking at the scrap of paper. I had held it so long that the writing was smeared.

4 to the right.

Four what? I knew it wasn't four steps. I had already tried that. Maybe it was giant steps. Maybe it was minutes. Walk four minutes to the right? With Goat it could be anything.

When we got to the corner, I was still looking at the scrap of paper. Four blocks maybe. No, that would put us on the other side of the highway. We weren't allowed to cross the highway.

"I'll give you one more clue," Goat said. "It's not four blocks. That would put us across the highway."

"I know! I figured that out!"

"So what do you think it is?" he asked.

"Houses maybe? Four houses?" I looked down the street.

"How could it be houses?" Goat said. "You can go four houses to the right, but how can you go six houses to the left? There aren't any houses there."

"No, nothing but trees."

Goat stuck his hands in his pockets. It was a quick movement, and it gave him away just as the flower had given me away.

I felt better.

"Let me see," I said. I started down the sidewalk. "Could it be four trees? One—two—three—four trees?"

Goat followed slowly.

"Six trees to the left. Now, what's the next clue? Seven across. Why, yes, there are seven trees."

Goat was following even slower now. "You didn't really figure it out," he said. "I gave it away."

"Well, so did I. You didn't even have to look at my map—just the old flower on the watch. Here we go. One ahead, two sideways. Look up. Aha!"

There was a small paper bag hanging from the limb overhead. I took it down and opened it.

Inside was half a package of breath mints, a Matchbox car with one wheel missing, and two bird feathers.

"How do you like your treasure?" Goat asked finally.

"Everything I always wanted, Goat my Pal."

"Look, if you don't want the breath mints, I'll put them back in my mom's purse."

"I want them. And if you don't want the knife, you can give it back to me."

"I want it."

I put all the stuff in my pocket, and Goat and I stood there for a moment. Goat looked down at his shoes and then up at me. "Want to do it again?" he asked. "Treasure hunt?"

"I guess."

"Maps or clues?"

"I'll do a map—you do clues."

"Fine with me," Goat said, "only I'm not going to give it away this time."

"Me either."

"Let's get going."

And we ran in opposite directions for home.

Chapter Two

The Hunt for the Chocolate Treasure

"Where are you going, Jackson?" my mom asked.

"Goat and I are having a treasure hunt. Here's my map. Last time I burned the edges so it looked like a real treasure map, but I'm in a hurry. I've got to go. 'Bye."

"You're not going anywhere." She got between me and the door. "You have to practice."

"Practice what?"

"Piano."

"Mom, I practiced!"

"When? Last week? Last month?"

"Mom, I've got to go. Goat's waiting for me. We had one treasure hunt, but it didn't work. So we've got to have another one."

"I'm sorry, but you need to practice."

"Mom!"

"Your lesson is—" My mom looked at her watch. "Your lesson is in one hour. You have not practiced all week."

She pointed to the living room. When my mom points, I go.

I sat down at the piano. I turned to

"The Parade of the Little White Mice." I began to play.

When I played, the little white mice didn't exactly parade. They stumbled around like the cat had got them. Sometimes they even rolled over and played dead.

The doorbell rang. The little white mice stopped.

"I'll get it," I called.

My mom stuck her head in the living room.

"Practice!" she said.

I played a few more notes, but I was listening to what was happening at the front door.

It was Goat. He said, "Hi. Where's Jackson? We were supposed to be having a treasure hunt. I got my clues and everything. My treasure is waiting!"

Goat sounded very happy and excited.

I rose from the piano.

"Jackson is practicing."

I sat back down.

"Oh," Goat said. "When will he be through?"

"In an hour and a half."

"An hour and a half!" Goat said. "My treasure won't last for an hour and a half. My treasure is the kind of treasure, well—let's just say that doesn't last an hour and a half!"

"I'm sorry, Goat."

"Well, tell him he missed out on something he really likes."

"I will."

"Something he *really* likes."

"I'll tell him."

"Here are the clues he would have followed if he had been able to. And if he'd followed these clues, he'd have gotten something he really, really likes."

"I'll give them to him after he finishes his lesson."

"That will be too late," Goat said.

Suddenly I knew what my treasure was. If it was something that wouldn't last, it was something that would melt.

I closed my book.

What could it be? Something that would melt—something that would melt—

Suddenly I knew. A chocolate Popsicle. I love chocolate Popsicles. Somewhere in some hollow tree was a chocolate Popsicle. My chocolate Popsicle! And it was beginning to melt.

"I don't hear you practicing, Jackson," Mom called.

I hit a few notes, like little white mice scrambling for safety. But all I could think of was my chocolate Popsicle. I wanted that chocolate Popsicle. I had to have that chocolate Popsicle.

I jumped up. "Mom, I have to go to the bathroom," I called.

I ran through the living room. There

was a small dirty scrap of paper on the table. My clues. I read them fast.

Sidewalk, left. Street, right. Corner, cross. Sidewalk, right. Halfway, up. Door, knock. . . .

I ran out the front door and took a left. Popsicle—chocolate Popsicle. It was all I could think about.

I ran to the street and crossed. At the sidewalk I took a right. Popsicle—chocolate Popsicle. Halfway down the block, I came to the steps.

It was Goat's house. I ran up the steps and knocked at the door.

"Who is it?" Goat's mom called.

"It's me—Jackson," I called. I was panting. The words beat in my brain—chocolate Popsicle—chocolate Popsicle—choc—

"Come in, Jackson. I don't know where Goat is."

"I'll look."

I went in the house reading the rest of the clues.

Room, enter. Door, right. Room, cross.

I entered the room. I took a right into the kitchen. I crossed the floor.

Door, open.

There was the door—the refrigerator door. I opened it. My mouth had started watering.

I looked in the freezer. There was the chocolate Popsicle—the most beautiful chocolate Popsicle I had ever seen in my life. I grabbed it. I tore off the paper. I bit.

Ah, chocolate Popsicle!

I yelled, "Mrs. McGee, tell Goat I'll see him later."

"All right."

I closed the door and ran out of Goat's house. I started for home.

I ate my Popsicle as I ran. I ate so fast my teeth hurt.

I finished the Popsicle as I went up the steps. My mom was on the phone and had not missed the sounds of the little white mice.

I ran in the bathroom and washed my hands. Then I went back to the piano. I was ready to play now.

"Come on, you guys, parade!" I said to the little white mice.

The mice were really parading when Miss Jones arrived for my lesson.

"That sounds wonderful, Jackson," she said.

"I know."

"You must have been practicing."

"I have."

"I think you'll be ready to play 'The Parade of the Little White Mice' in the Christmas program."

I felt good enough to promise anything. That's what a chocolate Popsicle does for me. "I'm sure I will."

The white mice were parading again when I heard someone say, "Pssst!"

I looked at the window. Goat was there.

"Pssst," he said again. This time he beckoned.

"Miss Jones, would you excuse me a minute? That's a friend of mine."

I went to the window. Goat said, "Mom said you came to the house. What did you want?"

"My chocolate Popsicle."

"Chocolate Popsicle! How did you know it was a chocolate Popsicle?"

"I figured it out. Well, you gave it away again. I heard you tell Mom that the treasure would not last too long. When I heard it would not last long, I knew it was something that would melt."

"I didn't mean it would not last long because it would melt."

"You didn't?"

"It wouldn't melt in the freezer."

"Oh, yeah."

"I meant it would not last long because I'd eat it myself."

I said, "Too late for that, Pal."

"Too late for what? I already ate it!" he said.

I said, "You couldn't have! I—"

Miss Jones called, "Jackson, I'm waiting."

"I couldn't help it," Goat said. "You know how I am about chocolate."

"I'm the same way," I said. "That's why I—"

Miss Jones said, "Jackson!"

Goat said, "I'll make it up to you. I'll write new clues, hide a new treasure. How long before you're through?"

"Thirty minutes, but—"

"Thirty minutes. That will be just enough time. This treasure will be the best."

I went back to the little white mice, wondering how Goat and I could both have eaten the same chocolate Popsicle.

Outside, Goat ran for home.

Chapter Three

The Hunt for the Stolen Treasure

I went out the door with my treasure bag in one hand, my map in the other. There was a smile on my face.

I was pleased with my treasure. It was an old Superman comic book, a fake ice cube with a fly inside, and four M&M's.

These were all things that Goat liked.

He collected comic books. He had wanted my fake ice cube ever since I had put it in his lemonade for a joke. And he loved chocolate.

I stuffed the bag and treasure in my pocket and set out for Goat's house.

I rang the doorbell. Goat's mom came to the door.

"Is Goat home, Mrs. McGee?" I asked.

"No, Goat has gone to the store," she said.

"I'll wait for him, if you don't mind. Goat and I are doing treasure hunts." I patted my pocket where the treasure was.

"I had to stop because of my piano lesson, but I'm through now and I have my new map and my treasure." Again I patted my pocket. "Goat is really going to like this treasure, Mrs. McGee. Don't tell him, but it's a comic book, a fake—"

"I'm sorry. Goat can't play. He's being punished."

"Aw. Why? What did he do?"

"Goat ate his sister's Popsicle."

I had that feeling of things about to go wrong. I swallowed.

"That wouldn't have been a chocolate Popsicle, would it?"

"Yes, and he's gone to the store to get her another one. He has to pay for it out of his next week's allowance. He knew it was his sister's Popsicle. I don't know what makes Goat do these things."

"His sister's Popsicle, huh?" I said.

"Yes, there were two Popsicles in the freezer. One was Goat's and one was

Rachel's. Goat claims he only ate his, but they are both missing."

"Oh."

"So you'll have to do your treasure hunt some other time, Jackson."

"His sister's chocolate Popsicle, huh?" I felt like a broken record.

"There's no need waiting for him. When he gets home, he's going straight to his room."

"Oh."

My chocolate Popsicle—or rather Goat's sister's chocolate Popsicle—had formed into a hard ball in my stomach. It felt colder now than when it had come out of the freezer.

I swallowed. "Mrs. McGee—" I said.

I was looking down at my feet, so she didn't hear me. She closed the door.

I rang the bell.

"Yes?" she said. She did not look pleased that it was me again.

"Mrs. McGee—"

"Yes!"

"Mrs. McGee, *I* ate the Popsicle."

"What?"

"I ate Rachel's Popsicle."

"You?"

"Yes," I went on miserably. "I got the clues for the treasure hunt. And I was in a hurry because of my lesson. My mom was listening for the little white mice. And so I rushed in your house and there was the Popsicle right where the clues said it was supposed to be, and I—I just ate it."

"Well, that was not very nice, Jackson."

"I didn't know Goat had already eaten his Popsicle himself. Honest. I just saw the Popsicle, and I thought, Ah, my treasure."

I felt as bad as if I had swallowed the stick along with the Popsicle.

"I'll go to the store and get Rachel another Popsicle out of my next week's allowance and—"

"There is no need for that. It was just a mix-up."

"Thank you."

"But next time—ask!"

"I will. Oh, I will. Is it all right if I sit down on the steps and wait for Goat?"

"Yes."

I sank down on the steps. I felt terrible. I always do when things go wrong and they are my fault.

Finally I saw Goat coming around the corner. He had a small brown bag in

one hand. He was walking very slowly.

"Goat!"

I got up quickly and went to meet him.

He said, "I can't play. I'm being punished. Some stupid idiot ate my sister's Popsicle and I'm being blamed for it."

I swallowed.

"Goat," I said, "I am the stupid idiot."

"What?"

"I ate the Popsicle."

"You?"

"Yes. I got your clues. I followed them to your refrigerator. I opened it. There was the Popsicle. I ate it."

"It was the ogre's!"

"I know. Your mom told me. I explained to her that I was the stupid idiot, if that makes you feel any better."

"It would have been better if it had been anybody else's Popsicle. The ogre never forgets."

Goat sighed.

"Well, I've got to go put this in the freezer before it melts. Then after supper, I'll have to watch Rachel eat it. It is not going to be a happy evening."

He started in the house.

I followed him up the steps. "Want to do treasures after supper?" I asked.

He shook his head. "Not really."

"Come on. It'll be fun."

"I've had enough treasure hunts. Anyway, something always goes wrong."

"What else could go wrong?" I asked. "Everything bad has already happened."

"I don't know—something."

"Come on, Goat. Please." I began to beg. "You don't even have to make clues this time. I'll do it all. I've already got my treasure—"

I patted my pocket and the paper rustled.

"And it's something you like—three things you like. Actually, it's three things you love!"

Goat looked interested. He glanced

at the bulge in my pocket.

Then he shook his head again. He said, "It will be dark soon. I don't like to dig in the dark."

"I'll hide it where there's light."

Goat hesitated.

"And you won't have to dig. I promise. Come on. Be a pal."

"Oh, all right," Goat said. "I'll meet you at the corner after supper. But if this doesn't go right, I am through with treasure hunts."

"Me too."

"Don't be late."

"I won't. And you will not be disappointed, Goat. That's another promise."

Goat went in his house to put Rachel's Popsicle in the freezer.

I ran hard for home.

Chapter Four

The Hunt for the Missing Treasure

"May I be excused?" I asked my mom that night at supper.

I had already asked this two times, and two times she had answered, "Not until you've finished your supper."

This time she just said, "No. Eat."

"But Mom, Goat and I are having a treasure hunt after supper. I can't use my map because Goat doesn't want to dig in the dark. I've got to make up clues!"

"You can make them up after supper."

"Mom!"

She pointed to my plate. When my mom points, I eat.

I finally finished supper and ran to my room. I got a sheet of paper.

I was going to do a clue that was really tricky. Goat would have a hard time figuring it out.

The tricky part was this: I was going to write the clue backward. Goat would have to look in the mirror to read it.

It was not easy. First I had to write the clue forward.

RETURN TO THE SCENE OF THE CRIME!

Then I had to copy it backward.

RETURN TO THE SCENE OF
THE CRIME!

Then I had to look in the mirror to make sure I had it right.

Right? It was perfect!

I was very excited. I put the paper in my pocket with my treasure. Then I left the house.

"I'm going to Goat's," I yelled as I ran down the steps.

I sneaked to the corner, going from tree to tree because I didn't want Goat to see me. I peered around the last tree.

Goat was there, waiting by the mail-box.

I ran quickly to his house and rang the bell. His sister, Rachel, opened the door. I was not happy about that.

"Goat's not here," she said.

"I know. I just need to come in for a minute."

She waited until I was halfway through the door, and then she shut the door on me. She did this to me a lot, but tonight—because of the Popsicle—she did it so hard it hurt.

I rubbed my chest. It seemed all right. The treasure did too.

"I know he's not here, Rachel." I pulled out the bag. "I've got to hide this in the freezer."

"You have been in our freezer enough today," she said. She gave me a look any ogre would have been proud of.

"Look, I'm sorry about your Popsicle. I really am. It was an accident."

She gave me another ogre look.

I said, "I just need to put this in the freezer. That's all. Then I'll go."

"What is it?"

I held up my bag with the comic book, the fake ice cube, and the four M&M's.

"It's a treasure," I said proudly.

"That is a treasure?"

"Yes. I'm hiding it for Goat. I don't have much time, Rachel. Please let me put it in the freezer."

"What for?"

"So he can find it. Look, I made a clue. Come here. I'll show you."

She followed me to the mirror. I took out my paper and held it up so she could read it.

"Return to the scene of the crime," she read. "Big deal."

Then she looked at me. "So?"

"So the scene of the crime is the freezer. That's where I stole the Popsicle from. I mean, that is where I accidentally took the Popsicle."

"You had it right the first time—stole the Popsicle," she said coldly.

"Come on, Rachel, give me a break. Let me put this in the freezer."

"No."

"Rachel!"

"I will put it in the freezer." She held out her hand.

"But I want to—"

"No. I do not trust you. I have not eaten my chocolate Popsicle yet, and it would be just like you to—"

"No, no. I would never eat another chocolate Popsicle from your freezer. Honest."

She took the treasure bag, and she

went into the kitchen, holding it in front of her as if it smelled bad.

"Thanks, Rachel," I called after her. "And I'm really, really, really sorry about your Popsicle."

"You should be," she said over her shoulder.

I ran down the steps and met Goat at the corner. He said, "What took you so long?"

"Hiding treasure," I said.

I rubbed my hands together. Then I reached into my pocket.

"Here."

I gave him the slip of paper. I watched him as he looked at the letters.

RETURN TO THE SCENE OF
THE CRIME!

"What is this?"

"You've got to figure it out, Goat my Pal. It's tricky. I admit that. Very, very tricky."

Goat turned the paper upside down

and looked at it. He turned it sideways. He turned it right side up.

"Maybe one letter stands for another one," he said. He watched me for my reaction.

"Maybe," I said.

"No. I can tell by how you answered that's not right. It must be— Oh, ho, ho. Now I get it."

Goat started getting excited.

"Already?" I asked. "What? I don't believe you know. What do you think it is?"

"I don't think. I know."

"Then what is it?"

"You don't mind if I go home, do you, Jackie?" he asked. He was smiling.

"Home?" I said.

"Yes, home," he said. "There's a mirror in my living room."

"What would you want a mirror for?"

I tried to keep pretending he had not guessed the trick.

"I want to look at myself in the mirror, if you don't mind."

He was grinning. I was frowning.

"You want to come along?" Goat asked.

"I guess."

Goat started quickly for home. I followed.

I was very disappointed. The treasure hunt had not lasted as long as I thought it would. It had not even lasted a minute. Goat had caught on right away. This was no fun.

I went up the steps to Goat's house and stopped at the door. Through the screen I could see Goat was already in front of the mirror. The paper was on his chest. He was reading.

"Return to the scene of the crime," he said aloud.

I opened the door and went inside.

Now the only fun would be watching him open the bag, watching him enjoy the comic book, the fake ice cube, the M&M's. The only suspense was whether he would share the M&M's or eat all four of them himself.

"Jackson my Man," Goat said, "the scene of the crime could be only one thing—the freezer."

I sighed.

"So, if you'll excuse me, I've got to go to the kitchen."

He went into the kitchen. He was whistling happily. I followed. I was not whistling.

Goat opened the refrigerator door. He opened the freezer.

He stopped whistling. His mouth fell open. Mine did too.

The treasure was gone.

Chapter Five

The Hunt for the Buried Treasure

"All right, where is it?" Goat said.

He spun around. His hands were on his hips. His eyes were slits in his face.

If he had been a real goat, he would have charged.

"That's not fair," he went on. "You have to put the treasure where the clues say. So where is it? What did you do with it?"

My mouth was still hanging open. I was more surprised than Goat was.

"I thought it was there," I said. "It was supposed to be right there."

I pointed.

"Where exactly did you put it?"

"Well, I didn't put it anywhere. Your sister wouldn't let me. She doesn't trust me where freezers are concerned."

"I wonder why," Goat said meanly.

I didn't say anything for a moment, just put my hands in my pockets.

Finally, Goat broke the silence. "Wait a minute. Let me get this straight. You gave my treasure to the ogre?"

I nodded.

He pointed to himself. "My treasure?"

Again I nodded.

"To the ogre?"

"I had to! She didn't give me any choice."

"I know," Goat said. He patted my arm. "She does that to me a lot."

"What are we going to do?" I asked.

"We're going to find out what she did with it."

"Right!"

"Follow me."

I followed Goat out of the kitchen. We marched in single file down the hall to the ogre's room.

From the doorway, Goat said, "All right, where is it?"

The ogre looked up from her book. "Where is what?"

"The treasure. You did something with my treasure!" Goat said. His hands were on his hips again.

"What makes you think I did some-

MATH

thing with your treasure?" she asked innocently.

"Because you were the last person to have the treasure, that's why. Because you were supposed to put it in the freezer, that's why. Because it's not there, that's why. Because—"

"Oh, that's enough," the ogre said. "Spare me."

She leaned back against her pillows. We waited in the doorway.

Finally Rachel said, "Maybe I did take the treasure, maybe I didn't."

"What did you do with it?" Goat asked.

"I did exactly what people are supposed to do with treasure."

"What's that?" Goat asked.

She gave a haglike grin.

"I buried it."

"What?"

Goat took two steps into his sister's room. Goat had not been allowed in his sister's room since he let the cat play with her Barbie doll heads.

Rachel yelled, "Mom! Goat's in my room."

Goat stepped quickly back into the hall. "I'm not either."

"Well, he was," Rachel said. "And he better not come in here again either."

"Where did you bury it?" Goat said.

"Listen," she said, "you two are the big experts on treasure."

"Rachel—"

"You find it."

"Rachel—" Goat took one step into her room. I couldn't help it. I did the same thing.

"Mom! Goat and Jackson are in my room!"

Goat and I jumped back into the hall. We gave some ogre looks of our own.

She yawned and went back to her book.

"Don't bother me anymore," she said. "I have to write a book report for school Monday."

She turned onto her stomach. Then she glanced over her shoulder at us. In a nice voice she said, "Oh, please close the door when you leave."

Goat said, "I'm not leaving until you tell me where my treasure is. I mean it! I am going to stand right here"—he pointed to his feet—"on this spot until you tell me. I don't care what you say. I don't care what you do. I am standing right on this spot until—"

Rachel got off the bed. She walked to the door.

For a moment I thought she was going to relent. I thought she was going to tell us where she had buried the treasure.

Then she smiled. When I saw that crocodile smile, I knew she would never tell. All my valuables—the comic book, the fake ice cube with the fly, the four M&M's—were lost forever.

"You kiddies have fun," she said.

And she shut the door in our faces.

The sound of our angry breathing filled the hall. Then there was the sound of a key turning in the lock of Rachel's door.

Then there were no sounds at all.

Chapter Six

The Hunt for the Garbage Treasure

Goat and I were sitting on the side of his bed, breathing hard. We had been doing this ever since the ogre shut the door in our faces and locked it.

Finally, I asked, "So where do you think she buried it?"

"Who knows?" Goat said.

"She's your sister."

"I know, but my sister's the kind of person who would bury it in the worst place she could find—a spooky cemetery or a bat cave—just so she could make us suffer."

"Well, she hasn't had time to bury it in a cemetery or a bat cave. It's only been ten minutes since I gave it to her."

"In ten minutes the ogre could find a terrible place, believe me."

"Maybe we should go out in the yard with a flashlight," I said. "We could shine it around and look for freshly dug dirt."

Goat thought it over for a while. Then he shook his head.

"Come on," I said. "At least it's better than sitting here. Maybe you don't care about my treasure, but I do. It's the best treasure I ever made in my life."

Goat sighed. "I care about the treasure," he said, "but I don't have batteries in my flashlight and my dad will not let me use his without a good reason. Looking for dirt will not be a good reason."

"Candles? You got any candles?"

He shook his head.

"None?"

"No big ones."

"Little ones? We can use little ones."

"Birthday candles, a few birthday candles."

"All right, Pal! Let's go."

I had forgotten how little birthday candles are. I was so used to seeing eight or nine of them burning on top of a cake in a bright, happy room.

One birthday candle on a dark night is not a lot of light.

We walked around the yard, bent over, watching the ground. We lit one little colored candle after another. We did not see one sign of freshly dug dirt.

Goat blew out his last pink candle.

"This is hopeless," he said.

We were standing in the last glow of my yellow candle when Rachel opened her window. "Having fun?" she called.

I said, "Rachel, can I ask you a question?"

"You can ask."

"Did you bury it or did you hide it somewhere?"

"I buried it."

"In this yard?"

"I'm sorry. I believe I said you could ask one question, not two."

She closed her window just as Goat picked up a stick and threw it at her.

"So where could she have buried it?" I asked.

"I don't know—probably somewhere horrible."

"Then let's try to think of the most horrible place she could—" I trailed off. I felt a stab of alarm.

Goat said, "Have you thought of something?"

"Yes, but she wouldn't—"

"She would too. Where?"

"I don't even want to say it."

"You have to."

"She buried it in the garbage."

"Yes," Goat said with a sigh. "That's it. The ogre would go for garbage."

"I hate to dig down in garbage, don't you?"

"Yes."

"But if it's the only way we can get the treasure—" I said, trailing off.

We kept standing there. Finally, Goat said, "What exactly was the treasure?"

"I don't want to spoil it."

"I just want to know how good it is. I want to know if it would be worth digging in the garbage for."

"It is a perfect treasure, Goat."

"It better be," Goat said.

He began to roll up his sleeves. I blew out my yellow candle and rolled mine up too.

Together we crossed the yard and went slowly into the garage.

Chapter Seven

The Hunt for the Frozen Treasure

Goat and I sat in the middle of the garage. We were surrounded by boxes, empty cans, milk cartons, newspapers, paper towels, coffee grounds, and grease.

We had dug through the entire garbage and we had not found the treasure.

We were sitting there in misery when

Mrs. McGee came into the garage.

"What have you done?" she cried.

Neither Goat nor I could answer.

"I swept the garage this morning and now look at it. What have you done?"

"We were looking for the treasure," Goat said.

"You arc to clean every bit of this up. Do you hear me?"

Goat said, "Yes."

"Every bit of it. And you are to help him." She pointed to me. She liked to point as much as my mom.

"I will."

She went back into the house. Goat and I got the broom and the dustpan and the mop, and we cleaned the garage. Then we went into the living room and Goat said to his mother, "Do you want to check the garage?"

MILK
Corn

"No," she said. "I trust you."

Shoulder to shoulder, we started out of the room.

"By the way," his mom asked, "what were you boys looking for?"

"The treasure," Goat and I said together.

"What treasure?" she asked.

"Well, I made a treasure for Goat," I said, "and I gave it to the ogre—excuse me. I gave it to Rachel to put in—"

"The ogre stole my treasure and buried it," Goat added in a rush.

"What kind of treasure was this?" Mrs. McGee asked, looking at me.

"It was in a plastic bag," I explained. "I wanted to hide it myself, but the ogre—excuse me, Rachel—wouldn't let me."

Mrs. McGee said, "Rachel, would

you come in here, please."

Rachel appeared in the door. "Yes?" she asked nicely.

"What did you do with Jackson's treasure?" Mrs. McGee asked.

"You mean that plastic bag of junk?" she asked. "I put the plastic bag of junk exactly where he asked me to. I put it in the freezer."

"Goat said you buried it," said Mrs. McGee.

"I did. I buried it in the freezer," she said, "under the frozen vegetables. Can I go back to my room now?"

"Yes."

Then Mrs. McGee said, "I have had enough of this treasure."

Goat said, "Me too."

"You boys get the treasure out of my freezer and be done with it."

"That's a good idea," Goat said.

Goat and I turned and walked back to the kitchen. Goat opened the refrigerator door. He reached under the boxes of vegetables and pulled out the treasure.

It was as pitiful as a frozen chicken.

Goat looked at it for a moment, then he opened it.

"Ah, Superman!" he said when he saw the comic book.

The paper crackled as he opened it.

I felt a little better. That's what a pal can do for you.

"And the fake ice cube! You gave me the fake ice cube!"

My heart warmed along with my treasure.

"And M&M's. I've never had a frozen M&M. Let's eat them quick. Two

for you, two for me."

I put mine in my mouth. Frozen M&M's last a long time, but finally we walked to the door.

Goat said, "Well, Jackie, it's been a long, hard day of treasure hunting."

I said, "It sure has."

Goat said, "But tomorrow, let's do something else."

I said, "Suits me."

I opened the door and ran through the darkness for home.